D1362986

THIS WALKER BOOK BELONGS TO:

_____

_____

_____

_____

For Lawrence Birley
D.H.

To Ian with all my love
M.C.

First published 1995 by
Walker Books Ltd, 87 Vauxhall Walk,
London SE11 5HJ

This edition published 1996

2 4 6 8 10 9 7 5 3 1

Text © 1995 Diana Hendry
Illustrations © 1995 Margaret Chamberlain

This book has been typeset in Stempel Schneidler

Printed in Hong Kong

British Library Cataloguing in Publication Data
A catalogue record for this book is
available from the British Library.

ISBN 0-7445-4367-3

Dog Dottington

Written by
Diana Hendry

Illustrated by
Margaret Chamberlain

WALKER BOOKS
AND SUBSIDIARIES
LONDON · BOSTON · SYDNEY

There were seven Dottingtons.
They lived in a creaking,
groaning old house and
they were all scared
of something.

Old Man

Old Man Dottington
was scared of the dark.

Old Woman Dottington
was scared of spiders.

Old
Woman

Dad

Dad Dottington was
scared of letters in
brown envelopes.

Ma

Ma Dottington was scared of noises in the night, and there were a lot of these in the Dottington house.

Joseph James Dottington (J.J. to you) was the eldest child and he was scared of doctors' jabs.

J.J.

Molly

Molly Dottington was the middle child and she was scared of water.

Hercules Dottington was the youngest and he was scared of just about everything. Most of all – his shadow.

Hercules

One day Ma Dottington said, "I should feel a lot less scared of noises in the night if we had a dog."

And Old Man Dottington said, "And I wouldn't be so scared of the dark."

"I suppose a dog might eat letters in brown envelopes," said Dad Dottington.

"And perhaps spiders," said Old Woman Dottington.

"He could have my injections for me," said J.J.

"And doggy-paddle with me," said Molly.

"He would chase my shadow far, far away," said Hercules.

APPOINTMENT
J.J. Dottington
11-00 a.m

So the Dottingtons went to the Dogs' Home

and bought a dog.

He was a large grey dog and his name was Hero,
so they knew at once that he was just the
right dog for them. And he was indeed.

He was a true Dottington Dog –
scared of everything.

Dog Dottington
was scared of
the postman.

He was so scared
of the dark he had to
huddle under Old Man
Dottington's duvet.

When the wind howled
round the house and
hooted down the chimneys
and slapped shut the doors,
Dog Dottington shook
and shivered.

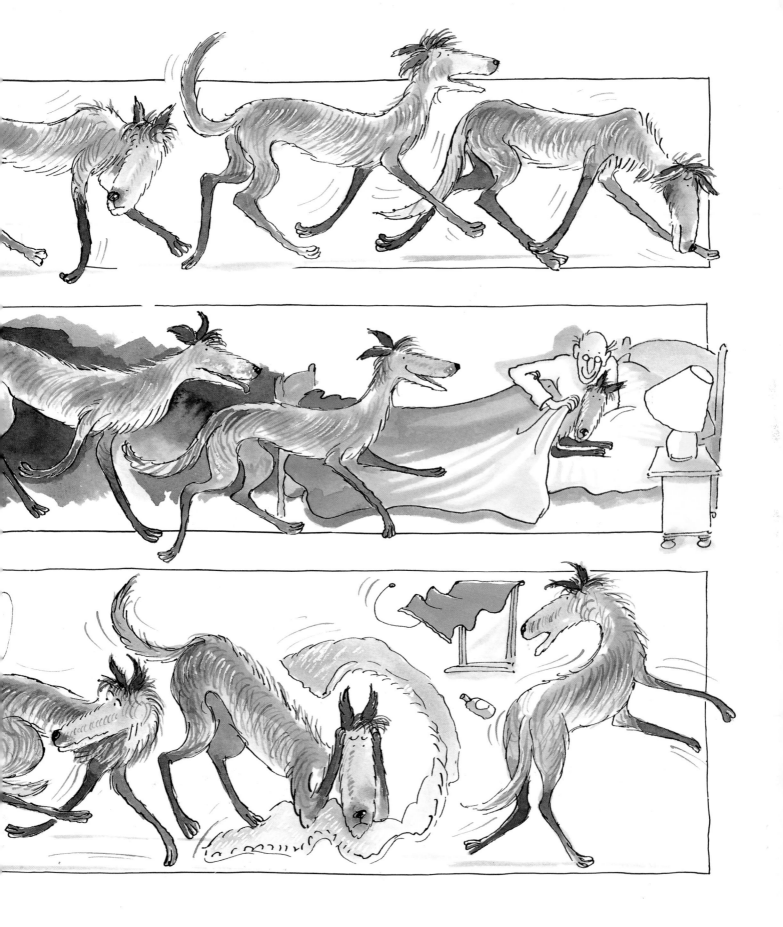

He wouldn't go near
even a puddle
of water.

When J.J. took him to the vet's for his jabs,
he drooped his ears
and trembled
all over.

And when he saw
his own shadow,
he chased it round and
round and round and
then hid in a dark corner
where he couldn't see it.

The spider who lived under the stairs only had to wave one leg to frighten Dog Dottington.

"There! There! You're quite safe with me,"
said Old Man Dottington
when Dog Dottington
huddled under his
duvet at night.

"Allow me to introduce
you to the postman,"
said Dad Dottington.
"Then you can carry
my letters.
They won't bite."

"Noises in the night," sang Ma Dottington,
"won't make us take fright!"
And she stroked
Dog Dottington's
fur because it
was standing
on end.

"Is the big spider scaring you then?" said Old Woman Dottington, when a quite small spider ran past Dog Dottington's nose and made him jump.
"I'll shoo him away."

"When the vet gives you your jab," said J.J., "just shut your eyes and I'll hold your paw."

"Let me carry you over the puddle," said Molly.

"A shadow," said Hercules, "is nothing to be scared of. Look! I can make mine dance!"

All the Dottingtons
felt a lot better now they had
a dog. "We'll look after you," J.J. told him.

"You don't need to be
scared of anything," said Molly.
"After all," said Hercules…

"You're our Hero."

MORE WALKER PAPERBACKS
For You to Enjoy

IT WAS JAKE!
by Anita Jeram

Jake is a dog and he's Danny's special friend.
He's also a useful scapegoat when Danny gets up to mischief!
This book is a National Curriculum SAT's reading list title.

"Full of humour ... great entertainment value. A fun book for
parents and toddlers to enjoy together." *Practical Parenting*

0-7445-2310-9   £3.99

FLOSS
by Kim Lewis

Floss loves playing ball with the children,
but will he make a good sheepdog?

"Kim Lewis draws the English countryside and farm animals
as well as any children's illustrator... A story of warmth and charm ...
with a satisfactorily happy ending." *Susan Hill, The Sunday Times*

0-7445-2071-1   £4.50

MORAG AND THE LAMB
by Joan Lingard/Patricia Casey

The farmer is concerned that Russell's dog Morag might
worry the sheep - but she ends up saving a lamb!

"A delightful story with true to life illustrations." *Nursery World*

0-7445-2030-4   £4.50